JOURNAL *of the* WESTBRAE LITERARY GROUP

Issue 4, Spring 2026

Berkeley, Calif.
2026

EDITOR
Jon-David Hague, Founding Editor

JOURNAL OF THE
WESTBRAE LITERARY GROUP

Published semi-regularly by the Westbrae Literary Group, promoting authors who bring fresh, raw voices to the forefront of American literature. We are dedicated to publishing work that challenges the traditional canon, offering a platform to writers with unique and authentic perspectives.

SUBMISSIONS

Westbrae Literary Group accepts rolling submissions year-round. We welcome work in the following categories: **Essays, Poetry, Art, Short Stories, Excerpts from Prose in Progress and Forthcoming**

Please submit manuscripts via email to submissions@westbraeliterarygroup.com. Include a brief cover letter and biography with your submission.

CONTACT INFORMATION

Westbrae Literary Group

info@westbraeliterarygroup.com

westbraeliterarygroup.com

CONTENTS

CONTRIBUTORS

Dave Anderson is a San Francisco artist who specializes in mural painting and planning as well as relief printing. His palettes are diverse, intertwining traditional and digital mediums.

Matthew Blasi is a two-time Pushcart nominee and has been publishing short fiction and creative nonfiction since 2006. He also publishes literary criticism and scholarship in peer-reviewed journals. Matthew lives and teaches in Shreveport, Louisiana.

John Allison Cannon approaches writing as a contemplative practice—a way of paying closer attention to life, savoring the natural world, and exploring the human condition, with the aim of adding more understanding and beauty to the lives we share. He holds degrees in English, law, and theology and lives in Lafayette, Louisiana, where he and his family enjoy the festivals, food, and people of its unique culture.

Timothy Dodd is from Mink Shoals, WV. He is the author of poetry collections *Orbits 52* (Broadstone Books), *Modern Ancient* (High Window Press), *Galaxy Drip* (Luchador Press), and *Vital Decay* (Cajun Mutt Press), as well as short story collections *Small Town Mastodons* (Cowboy Jamboree Press), *Fissures, and Other Stories* (Bottom Dog Press), *Men in Midnight Bloom* (Cowboy Jamboree Press), and *Mortality Birds* (Southernmost Books, with Steve Lambert). His poetry has appeared in *Roanoke Review, Crannog, The Literary Review, Crab Creek Review;* his stories in *Yemassee/Cola, Broad River Review, Anthology of Appalachian Writers* and elsewhere.

Billy Field is one of the last people on earth to see a meteor shoot across the sky on November 30, 1954, crash through Ann Hodges' roof, bounce off her floor radio and hit her on her buttocks, making her famous. Billy sold that story to 20th Century Fox. He has written for 20th Century Fox, Warner Brothers and the TV series FAME for MGM. He taught screenwriting and documentary film production at The University of Alabama.

Josh Greenbaum has been writing poetry and assorted prose-like stuff for decades, specializing largely in unpublished works. When not braving the streets of Berkeley on his bike, he can be found hiking, breathing fresh air, and cooking. He writes at the Left Margin Lit writers' workshop, where he is currently working on his first unpublished novel, an excerpt from which has been published in the *Journal of the Westbrae Literary Group.*

Mike Mandzik is a New Jersey poet, born and bred in the wilds of Essex County. His poetry has been published in *The Rutherford Red Wheelbarrow, The Journal of New Jersey Poets, The Stillwater Review,* Paulinskill Poetry Project's *Voices from Here 2, Humans of the World* blog, *Vox Poetica, Painted Poetry, Corduroy,* and the *Montclair State Quarterly.* Mike received an Honorable Mention in the 2016 New Jersey Poets Prize and was a 2022 Pushcart Prize Nominee.

Zach Wyner is a writer and writing coach who has spent more than a decade leading writing workshops in SF Bay Area juvenile detention centers and prisons. He is a contributor to *Tikkun, The Write Launch, The Good Men Project, You Might Need to Hear This, Your Impossible Voice,* and *Atticus Review,* among others. His debut novel, *What We Never Had,* was published by Rare Bird Books, and he is the co-author of the memoir *Don't Give an Inch: A Life of Activism from Berkeley to Palestine* due to be published this year by Iskra Books.

EDITOR'S NOTE

WELCOME TO the fourth issue of the Journal and nearly two years of Westbrae. Themes are not required for each issue but as the issue comes together, themes emerge. At least they do for me. Humans, we know, have a propensity to project their inner states of mind (subjective feelings) on the world around them. We refuse to exist in a vacuum; our minds are always directed at, or *about*, something else entirely.

The poetry in this issue beautifully captures this inward projection. John Allison Cannon takes the mundane act of grocery shopping and projects a raw, blushing passion onto a simple dragon fruit. Timothy Dodd directs our minds backward, projecting a deep, ancestral longing onto the fading ghost towns and cobblestones of his history. Josh Greenbaum looks inward at his own aging body, seeing not a temple, but a ramshackle house full of character, while Mike Mandzik traps us in the sterile, cellophane-wrapped confines of medical trauma, where the mind desperately maneuvers against physical pain.

Our prose writers push this concept even further, showing how we manufacture meaning just to survive the chaos of our lives. In Zach Wyner's excerpt from *The Vanishing Point*, a young man confined to a concrete cell, anchors his humanity to the AI-generated voice of his dead father and the lingering scent of a girl on a t-shirt. Matthew Blasi delivers a hilariously profound absurdist confession, wherein his narrator's mind completely disassociates to project a taxonomy of "evil" directly onto his own fibula. And Billy Field, staring down the barrel of a gun, projects an "x-ray vision" onto his attacker's tormented soul—a breathtaking moment of grace in the face of violence.

Paired with Dave Anderson's stark, highly textured linocut art, this issue is a testament to the mind's irrepressible need to orient itself.

Thank you to our contributors for sharing their inner worlds, and thank you for reading.

Jon-David Hague
Berkeley, Calif. May 2026

POETRY

John Allison Cannon

A Kestrel Has Come to Winter

A kestrel has come to winter
in this open field.
She'll seek out high places.

And the mice will go to ground
until hunger lures them
from their burrows.

And a careless few
will disturb the grass just enough.
And that will be just enough.

Winter calls for the wisdom of enough.
Of waiting. Kestrel and mice.

Ode to a Dragon Fruit

Dragon fruit—
blushing and lascivious,
pagan and passionate,
I shouldn't want you, but I do,

and I'm a bit embarrassed
to have you
in my basket
in line at the grocery store

for fear a friend might spy
a glint of primal fire in my eye,
or a stranger might ask,
"What will you do with that?"

or "What's it like inside?"
or think, "You don't seem the type,"
so I hide you
under a loaf of bread.

Torn

They've mowed
the field of clover,
torn stem and leaf
from the greening earth

with great rusty blades,
scattered scraps
of white flower
and left mulch
in ragged piles.

Blue moonlit fog
hovers low
over neat rows
of mower tracks.

And when the sun rises,
bees will come
to forage
and find
carefully curated ruin.

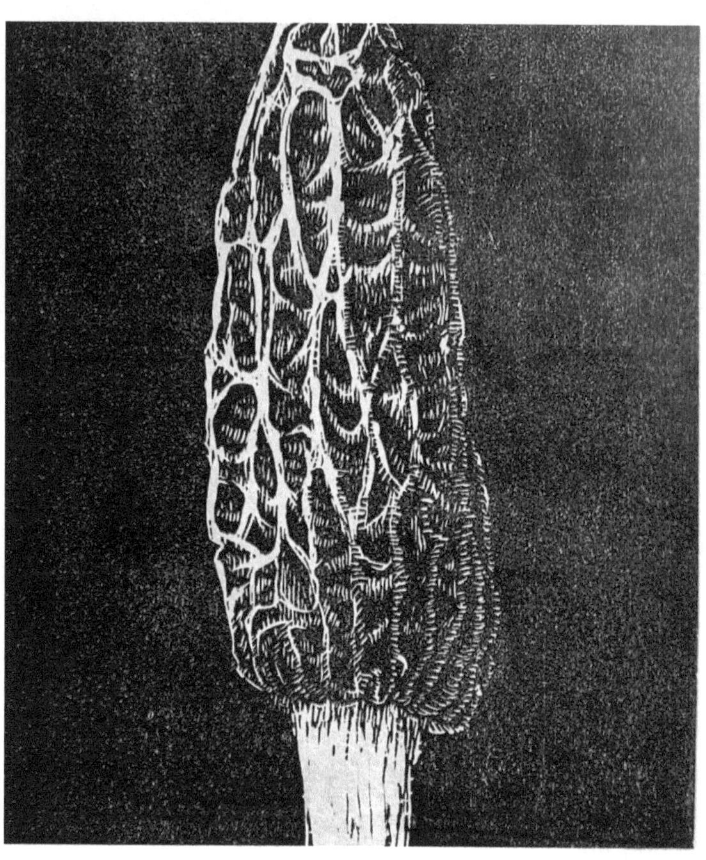

Timothy Dodd

Impasse Near Alderson

In the narrow valley, river-led, between two dark
mountains, the train's engine cuts, us, the tracks,
unmoving, candled toward a remembered dusk.

The hours shift blank, carrying a midnight mind
to basements bleak and banned, the wandering
coy between whispered intercom assurances

where death, my father, meets his capture, drain,
a heart failing and three sons childless, pushing
forward not the line ancestral, that it not matter

to me. Hours more and black snakes come crawl
through the carriage air, moments to Thomas,
great-great-grandfather at the window, long beard

the color of fog, hands turn like a window handle,
warped from farm work. In the glare is a slight
recognition, reflection familial, holding of doubt.

Onward we branch, neither knowing the other,
a family tree forgotten stead: shared junctions to

an open line, complimentary points on destination,

old shadows bend little to understand. Would that
we speak, but the engine sputtered, railcars jerked
and started, and we were back to lists of sought

for accomplishments, carried on our way to history
we can't discuss, opting for a silence of ambiguity,
unknown the blood between us. Dry and infertile,

a glass passage into time unfulfilled: short, unborn,
generations walled up to believing in advancement,
with dark stables emptying out their slow decline.

ancestral

Of the cobblestones, buildings that went
up in the days when my great-great-grandfather boarded the train at MacCorkle,
a depot now gone. And in the evenings

of cool weather, late October, of business
gone elsewhere, leaving in old doorways
quiet. Under the dark awning reflections
the lens—horse-drawn carts, bowler hats,

and sacks of grain, the room at the rear
of the hotel, cornbread, current of nearby
river, coal barges below a bridge of hand-
cut stone drawn by oxen from its quarry.

That I lived after the past and disappear,
looking at their steps, a range that lived
alongside ancestors here standing of me
on this corner, leaning against the wall

captured then, handprints of an earlier age
in bank vaults and stairwells to another
floor. They passed by this, us captured
in our acceleration and the memory gone

of her town warmth, the horses, pocket

watches, vests, when almost all of us came
from farms, and industry in the downtown
gripped the arm so that you never thought

we would ever leave, to become of evening
streets, bowed at dusk and empty alleyway
of warehouses, roaming into an absent night,
and in the wandering hills to find our place

in the ground, there he lies, and her, in folk
I come to know in the late breeze, and each
step here in the stopping of what is learned,
in the mind, and what it is that cannot depart.

Ghost Towns

In those little closets out there sitting in the fog
   no one knows,
lost centuries live not in numbers, but stare out
   from hillsides
moving off of history. Although we forfeit them
   in freedom

games, hero show, commercials, still I go searching
   in solitary
leafing, a jumping over of gun and engine, wanting
   my own
weight to locate the old crown, offer homage
   without the soft

flesh of modernity, away from sway of war,
   machine marriage.
Let me burn not found fossils, fuel, the meat in
   my backpack;
rather, a tightening of tongue, a reading of
   dysfunctional clock.

The new treatise is cold, in fact, and may bring
   exhaustion,
loss carried into nights without map, asking for
   salted popcorn

not ancient language. Doubts must come,
  the luggage left open

to Batts & Fallam, photos no one considers real.
  What remains
to breathe is posturing, a stiff, black and white
  contemporary
contraption burning but surface glow. You may
  leave past to rot,

its credit at the bottom of the hill, but another
  place comes
to life in the crash none care to hear, the future
  carry in lovely
ruins, moving in the trees, metal, cast, to cover
  our wounds.

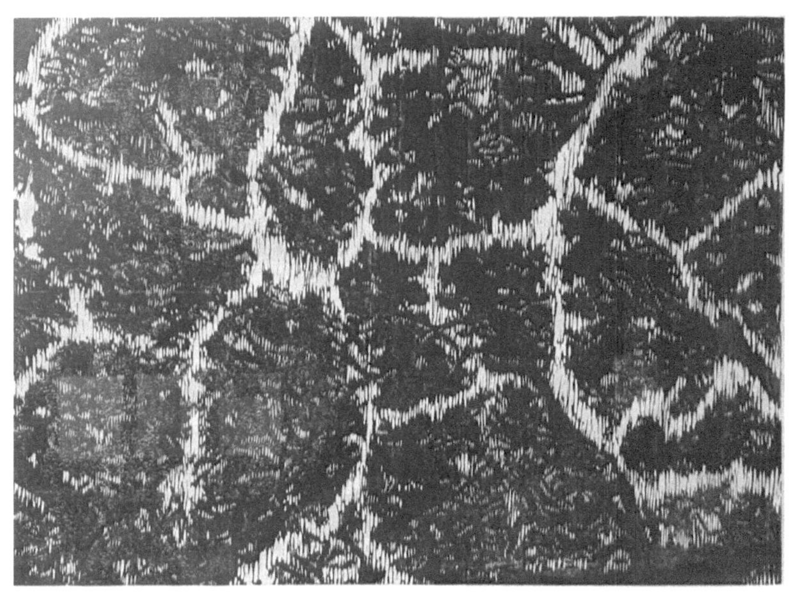

Josh Greenbaum

My body is most decidedly not a temple

My body is most decidedly not a temple.
It's more like a ramshackle house in the woods,
aspiring to be a cozy home
even if
the shingles are falling off the roof one by one,
and the doors sit unevenly on tattered frames.

In my house that isn't a temple,
there are no hymnals, only scars that have their
    stories to tell.
And crinkles around the eyes, and lines that nestle
    soft weathered lips,
ready to share a laugh
when it's time, if there's time.
And there always is, if we take the time to listen.

In my house that is no temple,
I keep the windows clean and bright,
so whether you're gazing inward
or off towards the infinite horizon,
The view is as clear as it can be.

And in my house, that may sort of be a sacred
    space,
the fireplace is ablaze with a warm glow, and the
    furnace rumbles softly in the background, ready
    to lend a hand whenever the embers start to
    die.

In my house that is, after all, just a house,
The plumbing works as it will, according to its
    wants and needs, but no more than that.
The floors creak, and tilt, and in the cracks
    between the boards,
the dust of the centuries has gathered.
And out of my home's larder
tumbles food for mind and body and soul.
And beneath it all clear water flows.
And beneath it all,
cool clear water flows.

Half Moon Bay One August Evening

There's a couple sitting on a bluff,
looking out over the vast expanse of ocean,
holding hands, not talking, watching the waves
    come in.
They've been there for hours, or is it days?
Waiting for the water to tell its secrets,
wishing the clouds would lift
so they could see the faint outline of a distant shore
that's only a memory,
or was it a vision they imagined they'd once had?

But even under the grey sky,
a sky illuminated by a setting sun still somewhere
    in the distance
so far away that only this grey-green glow remains.
Even under *this* sky,
as the trembling waves crash with their own grey-
    green color,
yellow criss-crosses of foam churning over and
    under them.
Even as the waves fall into themselves and melt
    into the soft white sand.
All at once I see it:
The sky and sea have become one, the horizon
    disappears.
The ripples in the water, the ripples in the sand,
the ripples in the patchwork green and yellow,

brown and white speckled shrubs and grasses that
    blanket the bluff,
are all enveloped by a fog that illuminates the
    fleeting light
still glimmering from a setting sun
still hidden deep in a cloud bank at the edge of the
    world.

And suddenly we're all floating.
I hold my arms out to catch the fog – and my
    wrinkled hands are floating too.
The couple stand and walk as though they can
    escape the sky and sea together.
And they too float in the sea of fog.
Only the sounds of the birds calling remind us
that we're still tethered to the earth.
That earth that now somehow floats
between the deepening fog and the grey-green sea.

Mike Mandzik

Still Life with Saran Wrap

How often have men escaped
from the pain of their own
bodies with the aid of that
sentimental aspect of the
imagination that feels the ills of
others' flesh as its own?
–Yukio Mishima

The swing of pendulating days
stretched clear to transparency,
folded and sealed with a neatness naturally
ascribed to habit:

    folded and sealed,

                unfolded and eaten,
a quiet arc of activity
enlivens the presupposition
of the prepackaged propensity
for the penultimate stillness.

    Used to excess: crumpled,

                thrown away.
Then, alive again with inanimate energy,

aching to open the numbed hand,
stretching to relieve the shriveled skin,
bending lightly, paining not to hurt:

  how to fix???

The mind's motions do but
little to relieve body stiffness,
to twist the unturnable.

1.
      Hour after
hour, how easily
we see
      the time depart.
All that has been given to us,
all that we have, we hold not.
To have not now,
      a supple slight of hand.

Time for pulse, blood pressure, temperature
to be checked, recorded, charted. But
            to remember that

all we learned did not save us,
could not keep us out of this hospital,
cannot keep us from seeing through this
routine, this ticking ridiculousness.

We are here, that is all we know.

After the unrememberable interminable night,
flashed of light, pain, equipment, doctors:
now feel the tubes running into your body,
now breathe the air pumped right down into your
    lungs,
    you are tied
    you have IV
    you have tubes in your torso, mister,
    you ain't goin' anywhere!

So,
what about Custer's Last Stand?
Who *was* the character who shot Lincoln?
Which president felt the need to torture Vietnam?
How many barrels of oil do I save laid up like this?
How many tons of grain?
Can it loosen my clavicle brace
if I answer correctly?
Will my broken ribs stop hurting for a minute?

2.

      "Time to bathe,"

                the nurse saith.
      Ridiculous.
                How do you bathe
      in a basin?

                        Can't even wash my own
    back!

I pulled the last Steri Strips off the suture in my
    stomach.
Scabs start to fall off. I cannot yet move my arms
    without the brace
scaping the skin under them.
                    How does this clavicle brace relate
to the conscience of our nation, to the Watergate's
    Milhous,
to Albany's true blue?

                    Our shoulders are all tied back.
        What movement we have
                        is muffled.

We do not see.

We are not seen.

Wearing cellophane clothing
bought in special sales for the soul.

The prepackaged emptiness,
unmitigated by my glimpse at a really big idea,
is the closest I will come to truth this month.

"He really doesn't have a temperature, it's
only 99.2."
Blood pressure neatly wrapped,
pulse caught in a fold lock top.
Stale sardines in soiled saran wrap.

Blackout

a river bed carved,   worn
along the banks,
travel has indented
soil to a point
   (to a line, actually)

            The surface of the space
dissolved describes a
     lapse
       in the memory of
surfaces—

             uncrustable dreams
      stoking faint musical hearths,

   baked by the blaze of uncountable suns,
suns seen so close together,
      the space between:

          darkness

            indistinct
              from
                light

Truth Is Beauty
and Beauty Is Cheap:
15 & 5 for a Room

eyes made to sing
fed from the hillfold flocks of folks

fat & solid as a calloused farm hand,

solid as a silver screen
    across which dances
    dreams & schemes &
    quirks of light.

            Over there, 'cross town,
            down and up the subtle stubble
            slopes of this mountainside
            municipality,
                    from the top
            of the ridge, you can see
            the City,   on the horizon

it's the edge of vision,
far as the eyes can reach they
    climb the stairstep skyline,
    glide over the reaches of Northeastern Jersey:
        the mass of trees ends   about where
        Bloomfield begins, and edges east
        over the Garden State Parkway east
        into Nutley; swing it either way, to

the north is Clifton, south is Belleville,
souther's Newark;
                              your eyes might
find a spot where the Passaic River
jumps out of hiding, or clears from being
hidden, by haze or buildings...
                                   the maze of

this panorama evaporates at

                              Night when the
lights burn holes of brightness into the
murky darkness. The lights cluster &
manage to muster most of the population, really
they do, there where the eyes can see, the heart can
dance, can sing of desire, of fulfillment, the hands
& head can make it,

              to the light, to the lady
              of the night, to her orange bed.

1.

                         Sexual deprivation
                           is cause for
                         consternation.
              Staring the arousal of
              foreign emotions in the face,
                 the fact of their terms, reeling
                 the mind, a rain dance of
                    possibility, of newer and bigger
                       highs, a haze of better action.
              Of faster footraces, the flow of

faces on the fluid pavement,
   verbal inundation wrapping
forgotten fantasies' anticipation
   in the fur of a March-hare's Maypole.

pretty maidens all in a row /
                              hardly so
on eighth avenue,
                    news-cast notice,
  typeset contracts,
                    get blown for gold,
"Goin out tonite honey?"

Such anticipation provokes
confusion unless You
look Her in the painted face,
the foxfur coat hot from the
holding company, unless you say
no or not so simply, yes, don't guess,
you get it now or never,
unless you lay in the teeth of
the queen.

2.

democracy's queen
is the whore of your dreams,
your kingdom of promise
influencing inaction.

            what fills your eyes,
            how do you focus the

> lies your experience
> lays in your mind,
> is there peace through
> the part your dreams
> take in walking sleep;
> do they drag on your life,
> are your feet cold?

she stars in a
skin flick, wind on the water
of freckles sanctity, speckled
titties in the grip of unconcern,
the pursuit of pleasure over
field & streams, over
the trinity of tidal waters,
bodies of the Passaic,
the Hackensack, and finally,
under the Hudson.

> does your lady wear
> a crown of wildflowers,
> has she captured the
> essence of such pacific
> pastoral beauty,
> does the fragrance of
> her own break through
> the garland gathered off
> the steeps of the mountain,
> the cold mountain of a
> solitary self, does the

                        touch of her adornment
                        greet you like a telegram,
                        singing?

                    and it's true, she can
                    tell you, the root of all evil
                    is in the lack of money, how can you
                    play if you don't pay, you *gotta*
                    hold up your end

3.

        the eastern union of
        opposites, conjoining

        looker limp &
        hooker hard

        broken treaty of
        sexual politics

        young man
        on a shopping spree

        she sells
        good time

        so you've heard.
        the resilient residue

        of all this hearsay
        has you clipping coupons,

cutting croutons for a
French dressed brain salad.

love hold me tight,
I'll fly my kite.

4.

so tasteless.
we watched them
take this body away
in an ambulance.
they carried it
out of a tall New
York apartment building,
and down the steps.
they wheeled it
carefully across the sidewalk
to the unit, waiting by the curb
quiet as a hearse. they put
the stretcher in and left.
Lola said, why dontcha gimme
the money an we'll get started.
I asked her if she
wanted some gum.
she said, yeah, it don't
come in strawberry.

5.

loving's art

heartlessly

bent, folded

spindled,
mutilated

its ring of laughter
like a cash register

but if the
truth it ain't,
the tooth it ain't either,
caried, drilled-n-filled

mouth full of
moon metal,

substitute silver
stuck in a hole,

love left   for
life   in a role

and the mask gone crass,
lines in the eyes

cracking

Prose

OLD
N°7
WHISKEY
JUST LEAVE THE BOTTLE

Billy Field

Dancing with God

43 years ago tonight
December 30th
a man with blood on his face
held a pistol to my head
the side of my head
because I had turned away from him
pleading with him over and over
that we weren't the ones who beat him up
but he wasn't listening
and I was backed up against a wooden fence
with no way out
and with the temperature at zero
I turned away from him
waiting for the lead to hit
and then
and I don't know why
I cut my eyes to the right to see him
and when I did
I saw him standing there
but I did not see the man who had
only moments earlier
twirled in the dark

and shot the pistol
that sent the flame
that formed a question mark
that asked me a question
and I answered yes
I saw that man
but what I really saw
was an x-ray vision of his soul.

This is the part where you say, oh no, you are making that up. It was an optical illusion. Whatever you wanna say, go ahead and say it. I don't care what you think because I'm telling you, and I don't give a damn if you believe me or not, I saw an x-ray vision of this man's soul, the same as if the doctor had taken an x-ray of your rib cage and put it up on the screen lit by the dim glow from behind, to reveal a phantom image of your ribs. And this was the same, exactly the same, except what I saw was an x-ray vision of his soul and he was warped and twisted and bent in terrible pain, and I was not scared anymore. Suddenly I felt compassion for him. This man is worse off than I am, the thought came to me, and I have a bullet hole in my leg. I stood up straight and looked into his face covered with blood from where the two thugs at the pool table had beaten him up and he looked at me as if he suddenly felt naked that I had seen his soul. He took one last look at me, then one step backwards, then looked at me again and took one more step backwards and then stuck the pistol in the back of his belt and disappeared back inside the bar. The two people I had hidden crawled out from behind the tool shed and looked like trapeze artists flying over that fence to get away. It was below zero. I knew if I bled out I would freeze and nobody would know I was there and so with a bullet hole in my leg and doing the impossible—but anything is possible if you want it enough—I pulled myself over that fence and crept around to the front of the bar, still cautious because I wasn't sure if he was still inside. But I had to go in, otherwise I would freeze and so I opened the door and went inside and when I did my *Boy Scout First Aid Handbook* came vivid before my eyes; "Get the wound higher than the heart," it said and so I laid down on the wooden floor of this New Orleans honkytonk and raised my leg and told this guy standing there to hold my leg in place and next I was checking to see if it was a spurter, a cut artery, when I saw this drunk who owned a famous restaurant running toward me with a butcher knife and I thought he was going to try to cut the bullet out of my leg and I shouted for him to get back but he kept coming brandishing that knife but all he wanted to do was cut my pants leg off to see if it was a spurter—and it wasn't. I saw a cowardly doctor, wearing a scarf with a piano keyboard design, peeking out from behind a crowd of people, not wanting to get involved. I got my medical insurance card out of my billfold and held it tight to my chest. "Take me to the best hospital in town," I ordered the people around me to do. They looked at each other. What hospital would that be? "I heard the Pope is coming to New Orleans next week," I barked, "If the Pope gets shot where would you take him? And this medical student shyly offered, "Ochsner's, I guess." And so the police came and then finally the ambulance.

Riding in the back of the ambulance, speeding through the narrow streets of New Orleans was like riding inside an empty beer can, rocking back and forth with a young trainee driving and an old trainer riding shotgun and when I felt us speed dangerously around a sharp curve, the old trainer shouted to the young trainee, "Slow this thing down. That mothafucker ain't dying."

Now that would be a good place to end this story. Yes, end on a laugh.

That way everybody will be happy and might like me. But the moment I decided to stop there, the spirit of the poem growled, "you left out the best part."

"I know," I confessed, "the part about the question mark made of fire," then finally adding, "I was afraid they might laugh at me. Say I'm stupid."

"Well hell, let 'em laugh. Who gives a shit? This ain't high school. And even if it was, who gives a shit?"

And so I said, okay, and I crept up on the story like it was this fragile thing that might run off if I pressed it too hard. And I began:

"I was a writer in Hollywood, and I had a story that the studio really wanted." But then I stopped still, not sure if I should continue.

"Go on," the poem said, leaning back in his chair, "I'm liking it already."

"And I was really scared that I wouldn't do good," I continued, "and this was my one big chance."

"Sounds pretty human to me."

And I worked real hard, intense, because I had no time to not be intense. And as I did, I noticed something happening that had never happened before, at least not to me. The words were moving around on the page, telling me where to put them.

The poem listened.

How could such a thing as words moving around on a computer screen be real? But there was no time to ponder such a question. And what difference would it make anyway, I said, stalling for time, still not sure if I needed to tell this.

"Cut to the chase," the poem barked.

I finished the script and I took it down to the studio and I sat in the hall outside the producer's office and counted the pages, making sure they were all there like a new mother counts the fingers and toes of her baby to make sure that, in the copying process, one of the pages didn't get turned sideways.

The poem nodded, the smoke curling up from his cigarette.

And the producer loved it. He said it was the best script that had ever been turned in, and for me to come in Monday morning and that he was going to give me another one.

And so I came up with another story idea which he thought was good and he gave me the go-ahead, "but you only have two weeks, this time," he made clear. I had had three weeks on the one before, and so I sat down to write and my job now as I saw it, was to make him happy. And as I did, I had a lot of fear. But fear makes winners, right? I don't know. All I knew was that the words weren't moving around on their own anymore. They weren't sliding into place where they wanted to be, but only where I hammered them into submission so that they might do right and make the boss man like me, and then maybe even make my enemies love me. I wasn't going into the zone on this one like I had on the first one and I didn't know why. I didn't even know how I got into the zone on the first one. I don't have much time to say this so let me go right to the heart of it, the truth I may be trying to get to—that on that first episode, I did something that let me truly and honestly see an x-ray vision of the story's soul. And on this second one, I realized I had never even gotten close to seeing an x-ray vision of the story's soul. And I didn't know why, but there was no time to think about it. My two weeks were up, and I had to turn it in. And so I did, sitting in the hall like before, counting the pages, the fingers and the toes already knowing they were all there, but counting them anyway, like counting them might make them better, might make them see me and how hard I was trying and how much I wanted this to be good and then in seeing that they might even move around on their own while the script was still closed, before the producer opened it. But they didn't, or I don't guess they did. All I know is I didn't hear anything from him. And then I heard a secretary say, "He came through here mumbling that it has a long way to go to be bad." And then trying to make up for it, not wanting to take away what small belief I did have in myself, she quickly added, "But that doesn't mean anything. He says that about a lot of people." I wanted to believe her. But I had heard the dog bark, and I knew what the dog was barking about, and so I did not believe her. I couldn't. It was much easier to believe the first part where my script had a long way to go to be bad, because I knew that was true and so I fell into this whatever you want to call it, this depression would not be accurate. To say it was this giant leap of not believing in myself would be more accurate. And then I did something that I didn't remember ever doing before—I decided I didn't care if I lived or died. I really did. I didn't care if I lived or died. Now, I know that sounds like a cliche and people don't listen to cliches, but all I can tell you is that that was the honest feeling that I had and that I carried with me to New Orleans two nights before the New Year's day when I went out on the town with one friend I knew and a bunch I didn't know into a bar I didn't know, not drinking at all, just waiting for everyone to get tired enough to leave. And that's when it all began with this fool getting beat up at a pool table by two cowards who ran out the side door just before the one who got beat up ran in through the front door, a black pistol in the right hand of a crazed man with a bloody face and a vision suddenly opened to me, an image of my father from when I was a boy, lecturing me, "if you ever go to a friend's house and he wants to show you his dad's gun—if you come straight home, I'll give you five dollars." And the image of him standing in my room telling me that came to me like it was happening right there before me and I looked up and saw a sign that said "Exit" and started toward the exit and the two people next to me, who I did not know, followed me down a hall and out what we thought was an escape, only to discover that the exit only led to a fenced in patio with a locked gate and a ten-foot wooden fence. There was nowhere to go. We were trapped. There was a tool shed that stood out from the fence. I got these two people and pushed them behind the tool shed then I got behind them. Suddenly the gunman ran out on the patio and fired the gun twice. I was wearing a white shirt and knew that if he saw me, he would start shooting into us and I would be the first one hit and so I stepped out to the side and raised both hands in surrender and said, "We're not the ones. We didn't do it." From the light in the hallway, I saw him twirl toward me and without looking, without thinking, and certainly without aiming, he fired the pistol, and when he did a bright orange flame shot out of the pistol as fast as the bullet and when that flame came out of the pistol, it, the flame, formed itself in the shape of a question mark and a voice in my heart, not in my ears, but only in my heart asked, "Do you wanna die or do you want to live?" And without thinking, I said, "Yes, I want to live." There was no question in my mind that I said that—I want to live.

And you know, the rest. I've already told you about me saying we didn't do it and then about me finally looking up at him and seeing the x-ray vision of his soul and me feeling sorry for him because he was worse off than I was and I had a bullet in my leg then him going back inside and me limping around to the front and the ambulance driver getting a lecture to slow down because "that mothafucker ain't dying." And it was all okay. The bullet went right between the two bones in my lower leg. "This only happens in cowboy movies," the ER doctor said. They operated on me. I was on crutches for a few weeks and then limped a while, and then after a while it was all over.

If anything is ever really over...

But I never forgot about the flame and the question mark and what it asked. I still ponder that. But I think right now, after 43 years tonight, I might have an answer. I didn't say "the" answer. I said "an" answer, and it wasn't an answer to the question about why the flame formed a question mark. I know what that was. It was a genuine, honest, and straight in the face question; do you want to keep on living or not? And I said, yes, never thinking even for one millisecond that the answer might be different. But the question I still ask myself from time to time is how did it come to be that in the first script, some of the time words would move around on the screen and help me see what to write next. Yes. I was working hard, moving forward because I did not have time to not move forward. And I was doing my very best on a brand-new word processor, one of the first in Hollywood and the words moved around on the screen and into the place they wanted to be. And they did it not begrudgingly, like, "You dumbass, you're so stupid. Let me show you." And then they would move. No, it wasn't like that at all. It was more like we were partners. These words knew I was working hard, giving it my best, and then it did its best like a writing partner, not like a know-it-all that was only helping out a fool so maybe this fool would shut up and stop whining. And so the way I see it right now, at least 43 years later, I see it like this; If we get up in the morning to write, knowing what we plan to write, but then when we sit down, if the words speak to us a little differently, the logic of our left brain might demand that we do that next planned thing…

But if we listen to the words
and follow them
and dance with them
to the rhythm of the story we're discovering
then in that dance
in the midst and heat of that dance
maybe that's where the story will let us see
an x-ray vision of its soul
and when it does that
we're dancing with God

no
hangovers?

Matthew Blasi

With Heavy Apologies to the Taxonomic Evil Enthusiast for All the Blood

FOR WHAT IT'S WORTH, I'm sorry about my fibula. I'm sorry I have in the past confused it with my tibia, sorry that, were I pressed to identify it on a chart, I could do little more than gesture vaguely and guess. And certainly guess wrong.

It isn't that I dislike my fibula. Quite the contrary, I think, given that I cannot identify it with any accuracy. I do not regard it as I do, for example, my ulna. I don't know what the fuck my ulna does but I'm certain, mostly, that I don't like it. The name creeps me out. Sounds like science fiction.

In the vast reaches of space, Captain Ulna . . .

The robots, led by Ulna the Flesh Chipper, rose up and made off with our cheese...

Or the radius. Or is it the radial? See what I mean? That speaks to its insignificance.

Digitals.

Femur.

Vertebrae.

I'm sure someone, somewhere, in some dirty hovel of the soul thinks well of them. But not I.

Coccyx. Don't even.

What a disgusting bone or, if I can pretend to know something about it, a kind of *region*, a terrible *space* that serves as an intersection of friction that is also, I believe, a kind of junction where bunches of bones, you know, are sort of joined? Or moving with less friction? And so forth?

Look, anatomy is not my strong suit. I'm also sorry about that. But I'm not sorry about *being* sorry about my fibula.

It's been a long time coming, this reckoning, this public apology. My fibula has been, will be, I'm sure, complicit in acts of shame. Do we need to talk about the bicycle incident? Do we need to bring up what happened with the above ground pool? My fibula can and will be identified, as it has been, in actions and events deleterious to good and moral living. I'm not inclined to dramatics but I am beyond confident my fibula will *always* be compliant with the forces of darkness in every possible way, on the daily, sold.

If you asked me, "Say, friend, don't mean to bother you, don't mean to pry, but is this compliance, this state of complicit engagement between, say, your fibula and the forces of darkness entered into *willingly?* I mean to say, is this cooperation with the forces of darkness and your fibula acquired through coercion or duress?" You would ask these questions evenly and with grace. I trust you. I know you. We have years behind and ahead of us and no one, not even my fibula, can take that away. But still, even with all the trust we have engendered with one another through, you know, things people do to engender trust with one another, whilst one of the aforementioned participants harbors the secret and horrible knowledge that his fibula is a thing of evil—even with all of that, the questions must come, must they not? They must be asked. Something prompted it, perhaps a pained look or a bad haircut or bruises where once there were none, but *something* came into frame and begged the question, and I know as well as you do that once the question is begged it cannot be begged off. From it, I cannot be rid.

So you will ask.

And I will answer: no.

It is *not* acquired through threats, trickery, or coercion. It is neither bought nor bribed, neither extracted through the deployment of violence nor the application of bad ideology, like capitalism... capitalism of the bones. It's given willingly, gleefully, even, and often with extraordinary delight. That is the brutal, beating drum at the core of my apology.

My fibula is *delighted* to be allied to evil.

I am jealous of the delight. I have never in my life experienced such delight and recognize now, as I approach the halfway point, that I never will. Such delight is beyond me. I have never so willingly entered into a compact (barring the loss of my virginity) that promised so much unadulterated joy of the sort that I would embrace without hesitancy the forces of darkness as has my fibula. But no, man. Not even close. This fucking bone has done more than me. I have to live with that. I have to live with *a lot.*

I digress.

With regards to evil, let me be clear: I don't mean taxonomic evil. Even if I did, I wouldn't be qualified to define that. I don't want to be that guy, that smug authority on taxonomic evil who goes to parties and tells strangers, "Hey, I know a lot about taxonomic evil. Ask away."

That guy exists. I've met that guy at parties. He came up to me and told me he had been thinking quite seriously about taxonomic evil and that his thinking had been both systematic and mechanistic. His terms, not mine.

I said, "Eh?"

"Systematic and—"

"Got that. It's the other part."

"Mechanistic. It's—

"The other other. My fibula."

This set him back which, in retrospect, was not what I had anticipated. I hadn't anticipated it because, look, it was a party and I was tipsy and busy telling people about my fibula and look. I get it. There I was and here I am, telling them and you about my fibula like a person who is by all accounts out of his mind. But I'm not. I'm trying to reason with the fact that my fibula has confounded me my entire life. It gets rammed into things, apropos of me, because what do I look like? Some kind of guy who rams his fibula into things like furniture and cars? Do I look like the kind of guy who careens about town looking for hard right angles into which I can slam my fibula? Am I a masochist? Am I the kind of guy who acquires velocity in his daily foot travels knowing, as the more desultory portraits of me have indicated, that I *seek out* obstacles? I do not. Am not. I am a man who lives daily with a fibula allied with the forces of darkness such that it, not I, seeks out obstacles, obstructions, protrusions, you name it into which it can be rammed, scalded, perforated, and the like. I live like this and not happily. And this greedy shit in front of me who had the gall to talk about taxonomic evil needed to know. He needed to understand. Except I said what I said and he said what he said and I responded and contrary to a default conversational trajectory, nothing was any clearer. I was, I admit, disarmed.

I said, "My fibula."

"Go on."

"Evil. I've been issuing an apology."

"Taxonomically or intrinsically?"

Son of a bitch. I said, "Friend, that way no sense lies. Or laid. Which is it?

He wasn't listening. He told me that he believed deeply and whole that taxonomic evil was a matter of great import and should be considered by those great and small, folks from all stripes, because wasn't the capacity for evil, much less taxonomic evil, in everybody? Didn't we all have inside of us a wicked little engine that could be hotly revved? Didn't I have that capacity? Didn't I hotly rev that engine? He bet I did. He bet I didn't just rev it. He bet that I left the thing in park and floored the gas. He bet I *liked* to see the needle shoot up the RPM. He bet I *loved* to hear all that goddamn growling noise.

I asked him, "Is an engine, this engine, metaphor?"

He said, "You tell me."

I said, "Do you live down the hall? Are you friends with, um?"

But he was not deterred. My friend, he was entirely *un*deterred. He was, in fact, anti-*un*deterred, completely around the bend. The fucker glowed. And I know that *he* knew that he had won. I mean he knew that right or wrong, whether or not his claims were fiction or he had gored me on a spear of ugly truth, I was left with no defense save defiance. I could defend and defend only because to rebut would be no different, nothing of consequence.

I began to understand, there with the music loud and my fifth or sixth drink in hand. My fibula was one thing, an affix of evil, tethered. But this guy was something else, a savant of taxonomic evil with no regard for the ethical integrity of those around him. If left unchecked, he—not I—would career about the place, crashing into the obstacles of ethical living, affirming nothing but himself and bones allied with the forces of darkness. I couldn't let this continue. I have always felt a sense of responsibility to my fellow man. I rolled up my pant leg. I showed him my fibula. I said, "This is real evil."

He said, "That's your knee."

I pointed. "Here."

He said, "That's your hip. Do you know where your fibula is?"

I said, "Not only do I know but I don't give a shit. You think you're so smart? What *is* taxonomic evil? Tell us all. I'll stop the music."

I had trouble stopping the music because my pant leg was rolled way up and I hadn't taken into account how it would impede my ability to walk, which was a lot, because it was really rolled up and kind of bunched into my crotch, plus everyone was looking at me funny like, "Why is he taking his pants off?"

I said, "I'm not disrobing." I said, "I was trying to show this guy, who's talking about taxonomic evil, my fibula. But I got stuck. Help."

They did not help.

I kind of made it to the stereo. It was off. I hopped around with the pants and leg situation getting worse and my crotch getting worse and I tried to see whose phone was connected to what speaker to stop the music so the guy who loved taxonomic evil could finally tell us all what the hell he was on about. Oh, I bet he couldn't wait! I bet I couldn't! I bet nobody ever at any point in time had flitted about with such joy and envy as to be me in that room with a guy who lived to talk about taxonomic evil and there was me, fibula exposed, crotch badly impeded with a lot of seriously crunched up pant leg, feeling as though I was on the verge of something like a stroke or birthday.

Nobody liked me hopping toward them on one leg even as I explained that I was mostly fine aside from the pant leg rolled up high enough to threaten my dick and balls and the pain *that* ushered into my life, same old, same old, and if someone would just point me in the direction of the phone or Bluetooth device that was connected to the speaker I could do what I had set out to do. Which was I forgot. I was hopping about and telling people as clearly as one could, given the situation, that my priorities had begun to shift from locating the music source to the diminishing integrity of my dick and balls.

That table came out of nowhere.

I came to in the back of a car. The taxonomic evil enthusiast was driving me to the hospital and said not to move because he didn't need more of my blood all over his backseat. Listen to me when I tell *you* that I told *him* that I didn't just bleed anywhere, anytime, especially in the back seat of a car owned by *that* guy who thought quite seriously about taxonomic fucking evil. No, sir. I had had *quite* enough of that in my life what with my fibula and the still embarrassingly current pant leg and dick and balls incident. I managed to look down and saw it was giving forth a lot of blood what with the glass in the flesh and I thought, that fits. Now I would have to apologize for all the blood it was giving onto the taxonomic evil guy's backseat *while* he was driving me to the hospital *where* I would have to explain to someone how I managed to injure myself and *why* my pants were threatening to impact my dick and balls, possibly forever, and so forth. Was that justice? Was that goodness?

I was deterred.

I was waylaid by myself. I saw myself outside of myself and I did not look good or even human. I was more like a dryer sheet with endangered dick and balls and a lot of red juice dribbling into the backseat of a taxonomic evil enthusiast and it did not feel good. I was also me from long ago, happier, better smelling, largely unconcerned with the fibula that was, even then, seeking every odd corner. Just to fucking remind me who was in charge.

Have you ever been scolded? Did your scolding protract over several decades?

Can you imagine the indignity of your own fibula scolding you for such duration? It would be, I imagine, like stubbing your toe, that small shitty one, several times per day, every day, every week, every month, every year for fuck knows. I'm sorry for cursing. I was upset. I still am. But then, I was *really* upset. I was face to face, red juices and all, with the reality of taxonomic evil and none of the pressure had abated in my dick and balls. I tried to roll down the pant leg. There was a shock of pain. There was a great gush of red juice. The taxonomic evil enthusiast screamed.

Would that I were quicker, younger, more effervescent.

The hospital was bright and smelt like new rubber. It was just me in the emergency room. The taxonomic evil enthusiast was gone. I kept thinking of the party that I had recently left and the glass table that had come out of nowhere. Was that taxonomic evil? No. Was it evil? Maybe. A variety. The rest could be debated at a later date. In the meantime, I needed to get stitched up and get back to the party to properly apologize for the destruction. I needed to apologize, as I have been for years, for the role my fibula played in the destruction of the glass table that came out of nowhere, total bullshit, and the blood that was surely on the host's floor and *definitely* in the taxonomic evil enthusiast's car, but also to use the opportunities, errant as they were, to prove my point. I'm sorry for my fibula. It is allied with the forces of darkness. At each and every turn, it veered me toward destruction, violence, and confusion. Its nature is nothing less.

The doctor or nurse or whoever the shit evaluated the severity and stupidity of injuries in ER patients came out and knelt in front of me and looked at my fibula which was, I think, trying to fucking escape what with all the broken glass in it and the bleeding, and shook his head and said, "It's only a Tuesday."

I said, "Is that a leg thing?"

"A what?"

"I can play along. Tomorrow Wednesday."

He said, still appraising the wound, "You lost a lot of blood."

I said, "Have you ever heard of taxonomic evil?"

He said, "You don't have to talk."

"Are you going to wheel me somewhere? I keep losing juice. What about Sunday? Do you even *want* Sunday? Maybe if you're pantsed and Church-bound or like to get up and do something dumb like run five miles you might like Sunday. But count me out."

As if on cue my fibula gave up a good hard squirt. There was maroon all over the whoever the shit's scrubs, the floor, me. Just all over.

"Uh oh," I said.

"Uh oh," said the whoever the shit.

"Gonna give a big old gush. A big honking squirt. You ready?"

He gave me a look. "Do you mean to say your leg or fibula is somehow in control of what is happening here? The blood, the gushing? Why do you have long, large shards of glass in your leg?"

"That's between me and the table that came out of nowhere." Squirt.

"Look into this flashlight."

"I have been for days." Squirt.

"We're going to get this glass out of you and then close you up. Hold, please." He stood, almost choked up, or maybe about to vomit from all the juices I was squirting all over him and the floor and myself, who knows or cares, but I was worried he would fall and crack his skull on the hard tile floor and then there would be two of us giving up the juices in the emergency room and then who would save us?

So I leaned forward and poked him in the belly. He stiffened. Then he, too, gave up all the awful juices. I think my poke had caught him off guard. It caught me off guard, too. I was giving up at a high rate. I was seeing stars. I was starting to wonder if I was going to die in the emergency room while my fibula gave me to the floor or whether I would, I don't know, get some goddamn healthcare from someone who could hold their goddamn lunch.

But that seemed to seal the deal. He started wheeling me to the back. He was talking about surgery prep and I was apologizing. I was saying, "I'm sorry about my fibula. I didn't know it was going to do that. Are you mad?"

I said, "I'm sorry. It's true. I'm sorry."

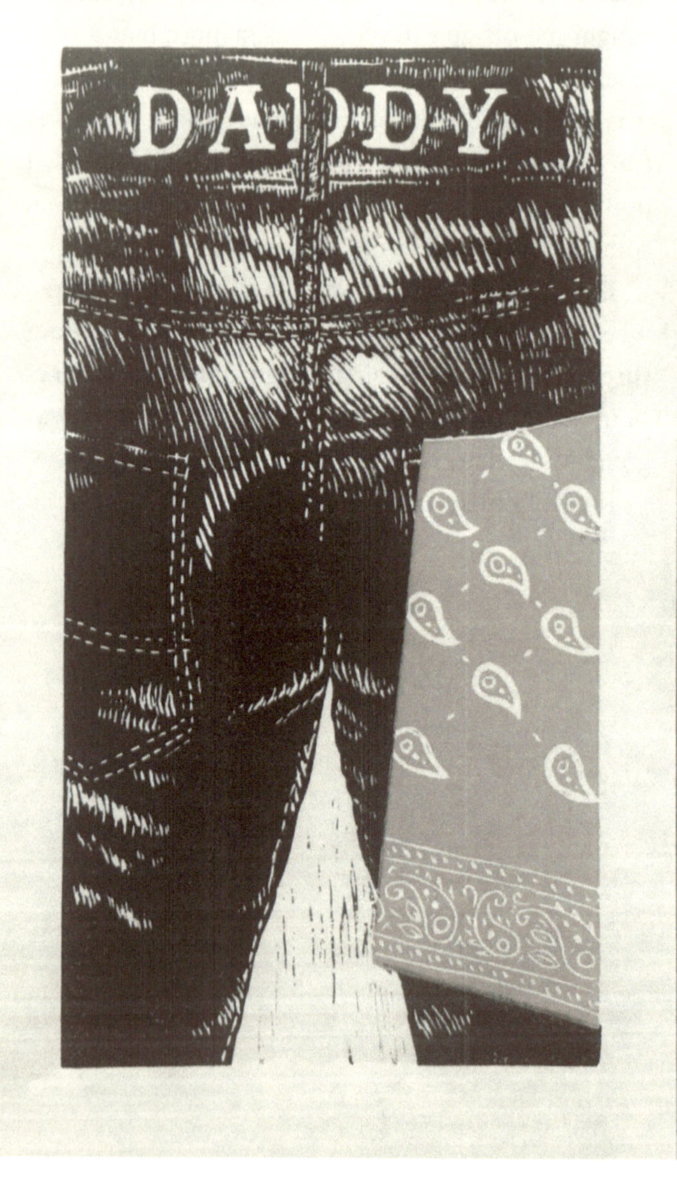
DADDY

Zach Wyner

The Vanishing Point

a novel, forthcoming from Westbrae Literary Group

The Vanishing Point tells the story of Evan Reverie, a teenager who has spent the bulk of his adolescence behind bars. Evan's world is unimaginably small. He engages with whatever lies beyond those bars through a state-supplied tablet, whitewashed history packets, old gossip magazines, action movies, televised sports and the disembodied, AI-generated voice of his deceased father—delivered directly to his ear via a piece of tech called a Guiding Light. What Evan knows of the world is its cruelty, and its habit of disappearing young people like him behind concrete walls. What he's just beginning to understand is that the outside world—of which he knows so little but of which he nonetheless dreams—is burning.

A 17-year-old victim of disaster capitalism the carceral state, Evan has cycled in and out of detention since he was nine. Ironically, all the talk of curing him of his "criminality," and all the attention paid to him by character assessors, counselors and advocates, has given him the notion that—like the celebrities profiled in the tattered gossip magazines he reads and rereads—he has star quality. When a reality television show called "The Vanishing Point" descends on his unit at the Haven House for Salvaged Youth, Evan sees an opportunity to show the world that he's more than a statistic.

Here, in Chapter 15 "A Tight Five", we encounter Evan locked in his room. Demoralized by his failure to meet the moment and stand up to a white supremacist detainee while the Vanishing Point cameras were rolling, Evan took out his frustration on Josh (a volunteer mindfulness teacher with whom he shares a real connection), shoving him to the ground and being immediately restrained by staff. Confined to his room, he reflects on his actions, realizing that (while he regrets having hurt Josh's feelings) the moment might play well for him, that his rough treatment at the hands of the staff could cast him in the role of victim and earn him more attention from the show's director. Evan senses that his time is running out. If he doesn't become a featured character on the show soon, the possibility of realizing the only life he's ever imagined will vanish. So, he uses his Timeout to rehearse a story he believes could endear him to a mass audience.

Chapter 15: A Tight Five

BACK IN ROOM 23, Evan stretches out on the cot, his hands folded behind his head, performing a smug, self-satisfaction for the camera in the room's upper-left-hand corner. He imagines Assessor Sessions on the other end of the video feed. He wants that man to know something that he's never had the courage to show him—that he doesn't need his approval. That, despite what Assessor Sessions believes about Evan's future and despite the outsized role he's played in determining whether it will contain any light, forces beyond his control—people clamoring for Evan's release—might reveal his power to be more limited than he thought.

When he was a child, just after the first laws banning civil disobedience were passed, Evan witnessed a massive protest on the road near his stepmother's house. To his child's brain, there was no way to wrap his head around the size of that crowd, or to understand what it was they were angry about and why it was they were blocking traffic. But he remembers their faces. And the signs—some of them on placards, others scrawled across torn pieces of cardboard. And their faces when they thrust those signs above their heads and hurled words like stones at the cops. It turned out their words were provocation enough because, before too long, the police opened fire. And Evan has no knowledge of how many protestors who fell actually died that day or whether the bullets were coated with just enough rubber to prevent fatalities, but he does remember the incredible surge, and the police falling back like fearful children in the face of a tsunami. And for a moment he lets himself imagine people believing that this story—his story—is worthy of their anger, and that someone might put his name on a piece of cardboard, hold it aloft, and hurl the name Evan Reverie like a stone at Haven House's formidable walls.

It's been a while since he's even thought about the Guiding Light™. He removes the earbud from its pouch and slips it in his ear.

"Hey Dad."

Evan! Evan, my man! How's it going?

"Fine, Dad. I'm doing fine."

You're back in your room earlier than usual.

"I got into some trouble."

Anything you'd like to talk about?

"Not really, no. I know what I'm doing."

You're sure about that? After all that time playing by their rules, keeping your chin up and your head down...

"You don't have to worry about me."

Yeah? Cause it sounds to me like you slipped through a hole in the ground and landed in your old self. The person you were growing out of and leaving behind.

Evan removes the bud. The voice doesn't understand. It can't know what's in his mind. That's okay. He knows what he has to do.

He climbs back into his aching body, adjusts his position, finds the sweet spot that allows him to peer out the looking-in window at a twilit sky—orange, brown, peach, yellow; colors he associates with cartoon depictions of the planet Mars. The ghost of Uncle Jeff's knee is still in his back, but the pain is diminished by satisfaction.

Melissa Moondive once said that the moment that launched her career was not the release of the hit single "Abuse Me"—despite the fact that "Abuse Me" went on to get more than a billion hits on StarGaze.com. She said that the single wasn't getting much play at all until she opened for Firestorm the night after she broke up with her agent/boyfriend. It was a crowd that she described as distracted, up until the moment that, before singing the song she had written for him, and following an argument that had seen the police called out to his house, she opened up about her ex. Several audience members filmed her impaling a floor tom with her mic stand and then sitting down cross-legged in the middle of the stage, head lowered, shoulders quaking. She stayed there for a while until, suddenly, she stood up and, her face a rictus of pain and streaked mascara, she told the audience about an abusive father she could never please and her subsequent search for love in unhappy, controlling men. Then she launched into the song, crying her way through the first verse before gaining control and building to the triumphant crescendo when she screams, "Love me, leave me, cleave me, bleed me!" The video of her performance went viral and, just like that, a star was born.

Evan knows that appearing on Vanishing Point is different than opening for Firestorm, but he senses that he's had a Moondive moment, that if the show decides to introduce him as a primary character and then builds to that climax—his standing up to a Line Holder, his victimization at the rough hands of the staff and his subsequent sob—he could become a someone. His cry may just penetrate deeply enough into the viewer to locate the place where their sorrow resides, make them realize that his pain is their pain and vice versa. His only regret is that Uncle Jeff will have to be the bad guy. Even though Uncle Jeff tries. Even though he's only doing his job. But, if Bret does his job well, it will be Uncle Jeff's knee in every viewer's back, and, beneath his weight, they'll all strain and struggle to breathe.

The intercom on the wall above his bed crackles. "Your boy went to bat for you," says Uncle Jeff. "That Josh fella. He begged us not to put you on a

Timeout. Insisted that he tripped. Said you never made contact with him."

Evan smiles.

"You can come back out this evening at 7:30 for an hour. You got to take your chow in your room though."

Evan rolls off the bed, drops to the ground and starts doing push-ups. While he's stuck in his room, he might as well get some exercise. Also, given that Bret is likely to be following him around in the coming weeks—learning his daily routine, asking him about his past—it'll be important for him to be as large a presence as possible, mentally and physically.

After his fiftieth push up, he lowers his forearms to the floor and holds a plank. He can go five minutes now without breaking a sweat. The only discomfort he feels owes to the cold, unforgiving concrete beneath his arms. He holds the position, keeping his abdominal muscles taut.

After a few minutes, he slips the Guiding Light™ back out of its case.

Evan! My man! Thought I lost you there.

"I wanna tell you a story."

Okay?

"It's like a rehearsal. You understand? What they call in the industry a 'tight five.' I want to practice it now so I can do it later without messing up the details."

Well, this sounds fun! I'm all ears, bud!

Evan sighs. Dead Dad is getting on his nerves, but he wants an audience, and if the Light could give him some encouragement, all the better.

"A couple of years back, when I was on home supervision, I cut my ankle monitor, left my stepmom's place, hopped on the metro rail and headed east. This was back before Aunt Carrie had moved out that way. But I knew this stat named Vince who kicked it out there. He told me about a party, said I should roll through. I figured that, after the party, I could hang with him for a few days, see what was happening in those parts, maybe stretch my stay a few weeks before coming home. After you cut that monitor, you know probation is gonna catch up with you eventually, so you make the most of the time while you've got it."

Well now, I can't exactly endorse that kind of thinking, but I guess it makes sense.

"Just let me tell the story, okay? I'll give you a chance to talk when I'm done."

Will do, my man! You have my undivided attention!

"I like the metro. I like watching the world go by, seeing all those trees. When I spend too much time at my stepmom's, or in Haven House, I forget about trees, about how you breathe different around 'em, even the ones outside the window that you can't lean back against and enjoy the shade.

"After a while, the trees got fewer and farther between and the neighborhoods we were passing through looked like all the neighborhoods that I'd ever stayed in. Wasn't much difference except maybe these neighborhoods were newer. Paint wasn't so faded. Wood wasn't so chewed up. Potholes weren't so big. But the trees were missing again. Just some raggedy-ass saplings here and there on the sidewalk that remind you of some Haven House newbie whose clothes don't fit, who looks like someone's gonna come along and snap him in two before he gets strong enough to stand on his own.

"I got to the station and Vince was waitin' on me with a huge grin and some new ink that he was dyin' to show off. When we got in his ride, he handed me a blunt and told me about this girl, Sylvia, that he showed my picture to. Said she thought I was cute. Then he showed me a picture of her on his phone and said she was gonna be at the party that night. He said we could use his room if we wanted to.

"I gotta admit, I was feelin' pretty good right about then. I hadn't met any girls since before the last time I'd gone inside—I'd mostly been keepin' to myself, too embarrassed to be introducing myself to new people while I was wearing an ankle monitor."

He recalls Sylvia in his mind's eye, summoning an image made hazy by smoke and drink and time. He remembers how smooth her forearms were. He remembers stroking them with the tips of his fingers and her laughing, saying he was crazy, and taking off her shirt. And he remembers how that moment seemed to play out in slow motion, lasting long enough for him to focus on each little part of her body as it was revealed—navel, breasts, neck, and then her lips reappearing as she leaned in to kiss him.

He shakes his head back and forth quickly, because the image is liable to make him lose his self-discipline. He raises himself into another plank, refocuses on his breath, closes his eyes. But her smile keeps flashing behind his eyelids like the afterimage of the sun.

You still there, Evan? If you give me your verbal signature, I can boost you up to a higher subscription tier and give you...

"No. No notes. Just let me finish, okay?"

Well, okay. But without the upgrade, I'll only be able to give you feedback on the first thirty seconds.

"The party was live."

Evan? Do I have your consent, Evan?

"No...just...please be quiet, okay? Where was I?"

You were at a party.

"And it was bangin'. Wall to wall stats just spilling out of the living room onto the patio, everyone dancing. Me and Sylvia weren't in the bedroom long enough to get anywhere before shots rang out and what seemed like a dozen stats dove in on top of us. While she was pulling her shirt back on, I was getting to my feet and peering out the door, trying to figure out where the shots came from so we could make our getaway. Then Vince crashed into the room, grabbed a shotgun out from under the bed and started yelling, saying he'd smoke any stat that tried to come in the house. I said that they were probably gone already, that it was probably just a drive-by, but he wasn't havin' it. He wanted to be that stat. To be powerful and dangerous and stomp around with his gun.

"Anyway, I told Sylvia to stay put and told Vince I'd go with him to take a look, and followed him out into the living room. There was still a lot of commotion and shouting and something must've spooked him, or maybe he tripped, but, out of nowhere that gun went off like BLAM!, lighting up everyone's amazed faces, and I looked down, expecting to find some piece of me missing, but I was still whole. Somehow, even though I was right behind him, none of those pellets hit me. Vince wasn't so lucky. All that was left of his right foot was a bloody stump with bits of his shoe and bone and blood so dark red it was almost black. I barely made it to the bathroom before puking in his sink. By the time I came back, Vince was unconscious on the floor and people were hurling themselves off his stoop like the house was on fire.

"I wrapped Vince's bloody stump up in a towel and tied a belt around his ankle but it didn't slow the bleeding. Then I heard the sirens. As they got closer, Vince came back around and was sayin', 'What happened? Somethin' smells funny.' Stuff like that. I was worried he might bleed out, but I wasn't about to stick around just so I could get violated back to Haven House, so I ran to the bedroom to get Sylvia and make our getaway, but the room was empty.

Evan releases the plank and drops again to the floor. He gets into a seated position and leans against the cot.

That's quite a story, Evan. I've got those notes on how to improve your hook. If you'll just give me your verbal signature...

Evan removes the Guiding Light™ and tosses it on the bed. He sighs, looks up at the unblinking eye in the corner of the room, and imagines a rapt audience on the other end.

"Sometimes, when I think back on it, I wonder whether Sylvia was even there in the first place, or whether I imagined her. I haven't talked to Vince since shit went down. I heard he's in a wheelchair. But, because I don't know any of the other stats who were there that night, don't know 'em well enough to be in touch with them in anyway, and because I ain't talked to Vince, I don't have much evidence that she...that Sylvia was real. That she wasn't a dream. Even at that time, the only proof I had was the shirt on my back. The shirt that I was still wearing when the cops picked me up the next day.

"See, after the shooting, I wandered the streets for a few hours but, without a place to crash, I went back to Vince's before the sun came up. There were no people around, so I ducked under the yellow tape, snuck back inside and fell asleep on the couch, my shirt collar covering my nose so I could fall asleep breathing Sylvia's honey.

"There's nothin' worse than wakin' up to cop voices. That's just about the worst feeling in this world. I woke up to two of 'em standing over me, laughing. They took me to a different facility—a place out by Vince's called Wayward Youth. When Wayward found out I'd violated, they shipped me back to Haven House. Before they threw me in the transport van, they tossed me my old clothes in a plastic bag and told me to change into them for the ride. And when I opened up that bag and her scent escaped, I knew she was real. That she wasn't a ghost. And that whole drive, I sat there with my shirt over my nose, tryin' to breathe Syvlia's honey so deep into my lungs that it might become part of me, like a song you can't ever forget, and anytime you want to, your mind can take you right back inside it.

"There are a lot of smells in Haven House, but they've all got edges. Hard ones. Sylvia's smell was different. It was soft. It was the kind of smell you want to get cozy with, that tells your body it can rest."

There's a knock at Evan's door. When it pops open, he half expects Uncle Jeff's tear-stained face on the other side. Instead, a disembodied hand shoves a fiesta bowl through the narrow gap and the door closes.

After forcing down as much undercooked rice and lumpy beans as he can, he lies on the cot and places a hand on his roiling belly to try to soothe it. The sky slips from burnt amber to black, but, like willful children, the moon and the stars refuse to come out from their hiding places. Evan nestles into the sweet spot on the cot and awaits whatever's coming next.